ROLLO
and
TWEEDY
and the
CASE
of the
MISSING
CHEESE

Laura Jean Allen

Harper & Row, Publishers

Rollo and Tweedy and the Case of the Missing Cheese
Copyright © 1983 by Laura Jean Allen
All rights reserved. No part of this book may be
used or reproduced in any manner whatsoever without
written permission except in the case of brief quotations
embodied in critical articles and reviews. Printed in
the United States of America. For information address
Harper & Row, Publishers, Inc., 10 East 53rd Street,
New York, N.Y. 10022. Published simultaneously in
Canada by Fitzhenry & Whiteside Limited, Toronto.
First Edition

Library of Congress Cataloging in Publication Data
Allen, Laura Jean.
Rollo and Tweedy and the case of the missing cheese.

    Summary: Two detective mice travel to Paris and back
in search of a valuable missing cheese.
    [1. Mice—Fiction.   2. Mystery and detective stories]
I. Title.
PZ7.A4274Ro 1983   [E]   82-47731
ISBN 0-06-020096-0
ISBN 0-06-020097-9 (lib. bdg.)

With love
to
Anne Ransom Dager
and her lapful

Tweedy was a famous detective.
Rollo was his assistant.
Together they solved many cases.

J. P. Cadwalader called Detective Tweedy the minute he discovered his Great Cheese was missing. "Come at once!" he cried. "Someone has stolen my Great Cheese!"

"Rollo and I will be right over," said Detective Tweedy.

"Who is Rollo?" asked J.P. "I want this kept confidential!"

"Rollo is my sidekick, my best friend and my assistant," said Tweedy. "No case is solved without him."

Tweedy grabbed his tweed hat and his pipe.
Then he and Rollo sped off in their red sports car.
The sun was shining.
The birds were singing.
They passed a meadow.
They passed a brook.

They came to a big house.
"Here we are!" said Detective Tweedy.

10

J.P. met them on the front steps.

"Who would want to steal cheese?" asked Rollo.

"The Great Cheese is five hundred years old," J.P. said indignantly. "The Great Cheese is very valuable.

Like my coin collection...

my paintings... and my rare books."

"I will give you a handsome fee and a cheese sandwich if you will find my Great Cheese."

"The cheese will be found," said Detective Tweedy. "Show me where you keep the Great Cheese."

J.P. led Detective Tweedy and Rollo to a door and opened it with a key that he took from his pocket.

"The Great Cheese is kept in its glass case in this room," he said.

"Hmm," said Detective Tweedy. "Are visitors allowed in this room?"

"Only on Tuesdays, when my house is open to the public," said J.P.

"Could one of them have stolen the Great Cheese?" asked Rollo.

"Hardly," said J.P. "Alarms would go off if the glass dome was even *touched*. Furthermore, when the visitors leave, the room is cleaned, and then I lock it personally. The key is always in my pocket."

"The room has no windows," said Rollo.

"Yet the Great Cheese is gone," said Detective Tweedy.

"We are dealing with a clever thief, a thief so clever," said J.P., "that he can disappear the Great Cheese from under our noses."

It was a baffling case. Detective Tweedy filled his pipe. "Here are crumbs on the floor," said Rollo.

Detective Tweedy examined them with his magnifying glass. "The crumbs are so tiny," he said, "it is hard to say what they are. But they smell like cheese crumbs." He put the crumbs in an envelope.

"Here is something else." Rollo picked up a piece of silver foil near the base of the glass case. "It says *Brie* on it," said Rollo.

"*Phe, phe!*" whistled Detective Tweedy. "This is a clue worth following."

"To where?" asked J.P.

"To Brie, France, of course," said Detective Tweedy. "Do you have a boat?"

"I have something better—a submarine!"

"We are off, then," said Detective Tweedy.

"Off to France," said Rollo, "to find the Great Cheese."

"The district of Brie is not far from Paris," said J.P. "My good friend Monsieur Chandelier, the French cheese expert, lives in Paris. We'll ask his opinion."

They entered J.P.'s submarine and soon were beneath the waves. They sailed all day and all night. In the morning, Rollo noticed a strange shape in the water. "Something is following us," he said.

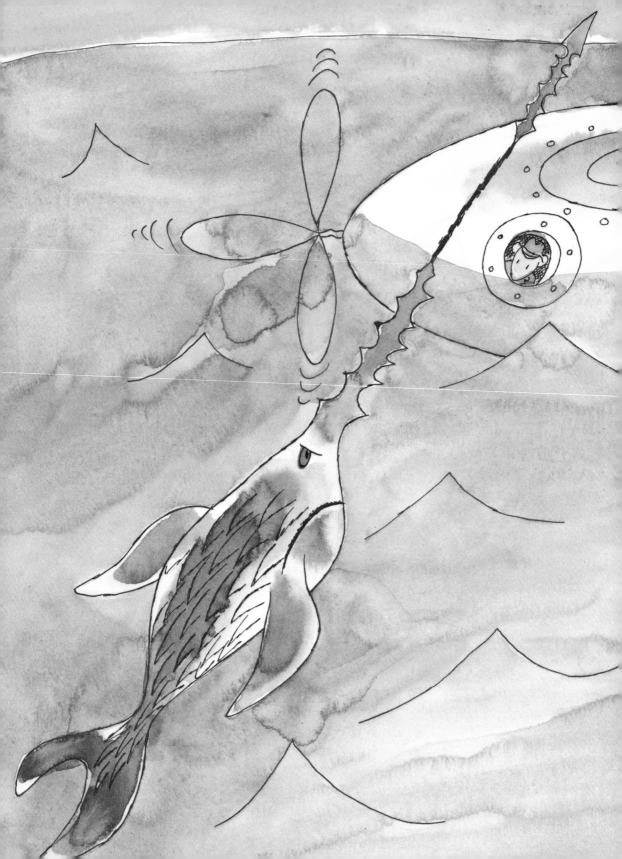

"It is a swordfish!" said Tweedy.

Suddenly they felt a sharp jolt.

"He is sawing through the submarine!" cried Rollo.

"Can you swim?" asked Tweedy.

"I think so," said Rollo.

"Certainly!" said J.P.

There was a fierce creaking noise, and the submarine
fell into two parts.

"Swim!" cried Detective Tweedy.
They all jumped into the water and began to swim.

"I can see land!" cried Rollo.

"This must be France," said Tweedy.

They began to swim faster. Finally, they reached the shore of France.

"Before we go to Brie," said J.P., "we must go to Paris and see my good friend Monsieur Chandelier."

"Is it very far?" asked Rollo.
"I don't think so," said J.P.

25

After they had walked for an hour, they reached the famous cheese museum. They went inside and met Monsieur Chandelier, the curator.

"Someone has stolen my Great Cheese," J.P. told the curator.

"Ze five-hundred-year-old cheese?" asked Monsieur Chandelier.

"Yes," said J.P.

"These crumbs may be from the Great Cheese," said Detective Tweedy.

The curator examined the crumbs through a powerful magnifying glass. "*Non!*" he said. "Ve can safely say zat zeze crumbs do not come from ze Great Cheese!"

"How can you tell?" asked Detective Tweedy.

"Zey *are* cheese crumbs but zey are *not* five hundred years old. And *regardez!*" said the curator. "A pumpernickel seed!"

"From the cheese?" asked Rollo.

"*Non!* From ze bread!"

"A sandwich!" cried Rollo.

"Brilliant!" said Detective Tweedy.

"From the thief's lunch," said Rollo.

"I see it all now," said Detective Tweedy. "We must return at once."

J.P. snapped his fingers. "We will charter a plane," he said.

J.P. himself piloted the small seaplane all the way to his dock.

"I am becoming impatient," J.P. said when they landed. "All this running about and losing my fine submarine. I want my Great Cheese back under its glass dome!"

"I have one more question," said Detective Tweedy. "You told me that the room where the Great Cheese is kept, is cleaned on Tuesdays after the visitors leave. Is the floor vacuumed?"

"Yes."

"In that case," said Detective Tweedy, "we should not have found cheese and bread crumbs on Wednesday. The room was locked from the outside. The thief is still inside the locked room."

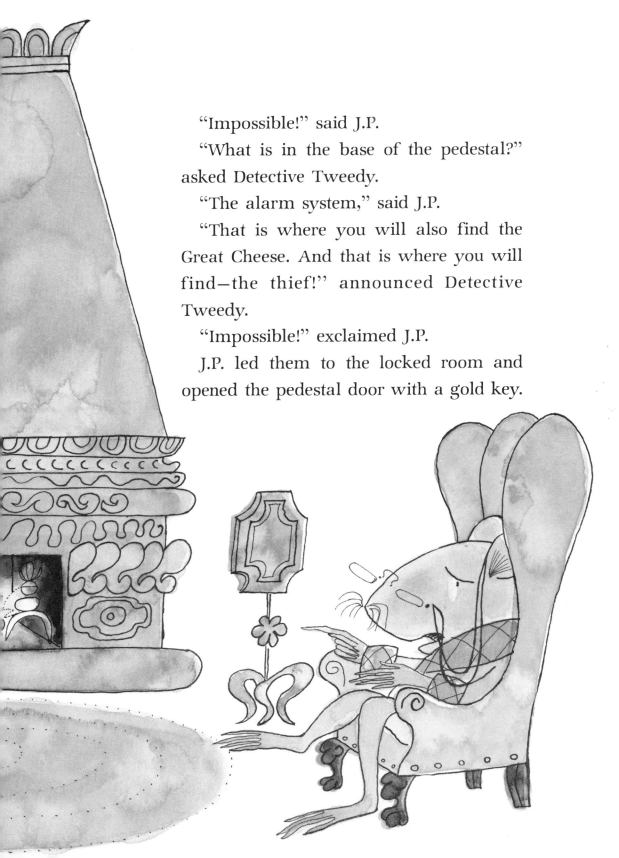

"Impossible!" said J.P.

"What is in the base of the pedestal?" asked Detective Tweedy.

"The alarm system," said J.P.

"That is where you will also find the Great Cheese. And that is where you will find—the thief!" announced Detective Tweedy.

"Impossible!" exclaimed J.P.

J.P. led them to the locked room and opened the pedestal door with a gold key.

A well-dressed mouse was seated at a small, elegant table. The Great Cheese was on a plate before him. The mouse wore a napkin around his neck and held a knife and fork.

"Good evening," he said.

"How dare you eat my Great Cheese?" shouted J.P.

"I was not exactly eating the Great Cheese," said the mouse.

"Indeed?" said J.P. "Then what are you doing in my pedestal disappearing my priceless cheese?"

"I was merely *looking* at your Great Cheese and thinking how good it would taste," said the mouse. "I am a cheese expert! Like you, I follow cheese auctions all over the world."

"Then why did you not bid on the Great Cheese yourself?"

"Alas! I am a cheese lover, but a penniless one."

"Well, I am not running a hotel for cheese lovers. Arrest the thief!"

"On what charge?" asked Detective Tweedy. "Your Great Cheese is not missing."

"I do no harm," said the mouse.

"Is that so?" shouted J.P. "Thanks to you, my submarine lies in two pieces at the bottom of the ocean."

"Your Great Cheese was always safe with me," said the mouse. "While I was contemplating the Great Cheese, I was actually eating—"

"A humble Brie which you took from J.P.'s kitchen," said Detective Tweedy.

"How did you know?" asked the mouse.

"You left some evidence," said Detective Tweedy.

"Careless of me," said the mouse.

"How did you do it?" asked Rollo.

"On Tuesdays, when the door was opened, I would slip into the kitchen, find some food, and get back into the room before the door was locked at four."

"Clever!" said Detective Tweedy. "How did you manage to make the Great Cheese disappear?"

"First I disconnected the alarm system and sawed a perfect circle around the Great Cheese. Then I created a dumbwaiter on which I could lower and raise the Great Cheese. But this time my rope broke, and I was unable to repair it in time to raise the Great Cheese to the glass dome again."

"Humph!" said J.P. "You may be a clever thief, but you won't get away with it."

"Don't be too hard on him," said Rollo.

"He seems like a good fellow," said Detective Tweedy.

"Did the knife and fork frighten you?" asked the mouse. "I was only *imagining* how wonderful such a cheese would taste."

"It *would* be wonderful," admitted J.P., stroking his chin. He paced up and down. "Well, at least you did not eat my Great Cheese! You have given me a bad turn, Thief, but you are a mouse after my own heart. I am as curious about the Great Cheese as you are. Let us eat it!"

J.P. and the thief and Rollo and Tweedy sat down to a feast. They all raised their glasses and drank to the Great Cheese.

"Cheeses are to be eaten," said J.P. "To the greatest cheese in the world!"

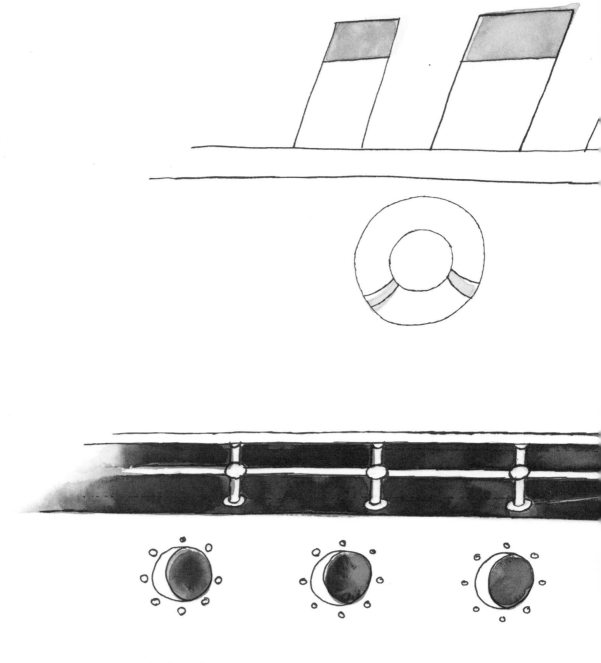

J.P. and the thief became fast friends and traveled all over the world in search of other great cheeses.

And true to his word, J.P. gave Rollo and Tweedy a handsome reward and a cheese sandwich.

DATE DUE
